MARGARET McALLISTER is an award-winning author who comes from the north-east of England. Before writing full-time she taught drama and dance, cleaned churches and worked in a retreat house. She lives in Northumberland with her husband Tony and has three grown-up children. *15 Things Not To Do With a Baby* is her first book for Frances Lincoln.

HOLLY STERLING was born in Dublin and grew up in southern England. She studied Illustration and Design at the University of Sunderland, graduating with first class Honours. In 2013 she gained a Master of Fine Art with Distinction from Edinburgh College of Art, and in the same year she was Highly Commended for the Macmillan Illustration Prize and was a winner of the Seven Stories/Frances Lincoln Illustration Competition. Holly also competes for her country in karate; she is a double National Champion and Gold, Silver and Bronze medallist at World and European Championships. She lives in Sunderland. This is her first published picture book. Her second book, *Hiccups,* will be published by Frances Lincoln in 2016.

For all the Allison family, with love and thanks — M.M.

To my Grandad, who encouraged me to draw — H.S.

The baby in this book could be a boy or a girl. We have
talked about the baby as 'him', but if your baby is a
girl you could say 'her' when you read the story.

JANETTA OTTER-BARRY BOOKS

Text copyright © Margaret McAllister 2015
Illustrations copyright © Holly Sterling 2015
The rights of Margaret McAllister and Holly Sterling to be identified respectively
as the author and illustrator of this work have been asserted by them in accordance
with the Copyright, Designs and Patents Act, 1988 (United Kingdom).

First published in Great Britain and the USA in 2015 by
Frances Lincoln Children's Books
First paperback edition published in Great Britain and the USA in 2016 by
Frances Lincoln Children's Books, 74-77 White Lion Street, London N1 9PF
www.franceslincoln.com

A CIP catalogue record for this book is available from the British Library.

ISBN 978-1-84780-753-3

Illustrated with watercolour, pencil and 'printed' textures.

Printed in China

1 3 5 7 9 8 6 4 2

15 things NOT to do with a baby

Margaret McAllister

Illustrated by Holly Sterling

Frances Lincoln
Children's Books

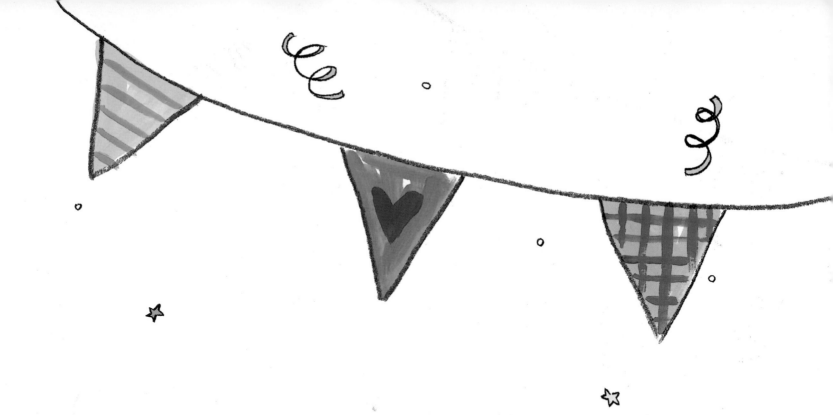

Congratulations!

You now have a baby in your family.

You will make each other very happy,

but you must remember these simple rules.

Don't...

play the **trumpet** when
the baby's trying to sleep,

or send him to play
with an **elephant**.

Don't...

peg the baby on the
washing line,

or send him up in a
hot air balloon.

Don't...

let the baby bake his own
birthday cake.

Don't...

give the baby to a
kangaroo,

or wrap him in **brown paper** and post him.

Don't...

plant your baby in the **garden**,

then **forget** where you left him.

Don't...

leave the baby in a
chocolate shop,

or let him help you **paint a picture**.

Don't...

give the baby to an **octopus** to cuddle.

Don't...

take the baby to **school**

or swap him for the school **guinea pig.**

Don't...

let the baby take the
dog for a walk.

Do...

cuddle your baby,

give him a kiss,

sing to him,

make him laugh,

play with your baby,

read to him,

and most of all...

give your baby
lots and lots
of love.

Also illustrated by Holly Sterling for
FRANCES LINCOLN CHILDREN'S BOOKS

HICCUPS!
Holly Sterling

How do you stop the hiccups?

Find out what happens when Ruby's puppy Oscar gets the hiccups.
Ruby tries all kinds of things, from hoppity-hop and slurpity-slurp
to her special magic spell. But nothing seems to work… !

ISBN: 978-1-84780-674-1

Frances Lincoln titles are available from all good bookshops.
You can also buy books and find out more about your favourite titles,
authors and illustrators on our website: www.franceslincoln.com

dabble lab

SHOOT EPIC SHORT DOCUMENTARIES

Thomas Kingsley Troupe

Raintree is an imprint of Capstone Global Library Limited, a company incorporated in England and Wales having its registered office at 264 Banbury Road, Oxford, OX2 7DY – Registered company number: 6695582

www.raintree.co.uk
myorders@raintree.co.uk

Edited by Shelly Lyons
Designed by Sarah Bennett
Original illustrations © Capstone Global Library Limited 2020
Picture research by Morgan Walters
Production by Katy LaVigne
Originated by Capstone Global Library Ltd
Printed and bound in India

978 1 4747 8737 6 (hardback)
978 1 4747 6797 2 (paperback)

British Library Cataloguing in Publication Data
A full catalogue record for this book is available from the British Library.

Acknowledgements
We would like to thank the following for permission to reproduce photographs: All photos by Capstone Studio, Karon Dubke, except: iStockphoto: FatCamera, 32; Shutterstock: Arvind Balaraman, 11, Astarina, design element, Becris, design element, bonandbon, 8, Can Yesil, design element, Darcraft, design element, David Porras, bottom 9, Grisha Bruev, Cover, handini_atmodiwiryo, (books) 26 Havoc, bottom 39, hxdbzxy, top 22, Jason Korbol, top 39, Kzenon, 19, Lightspring, background 45, Lisa F. Young, 13, Luigi Bertello, 15, MIKHAIL GRACHIKOV, cover, Monkey Business Images, top 9, Natasha Pankina, design element, Naumenko Aleksandr, spread 22-23, pixelheadphoto digitalskillet, 18, PK Studio, 12, Ramona Kaulitzki, 16, Seth Gallmeyer, design element, Shorena Tedliashvili, design element, silm, design element, vector illustration, design element, Vissay, bottom 45, www.hollandfoto.net, 21, yanin kongurai, 11

Every effort has been made to contact copyright holders of material reproduced in this book. Any omissions will be rectified in subsequent printings if notice is given to the publisher.

All the internet addresses (URLs) given in this book were valid at the time of going to press. However, due to the dynamic nature of the internet, some addresses may have changed, or sites may have changed or ceased to exist since publication. While the author and publisher regret any inconvenience this may cause readers, no responsibility for any such changes can be accepted by either the author or the publisher.

CONTENTS

What's up, doc(umentary)?

A local hero tells the story of how he saved a family from a car after it had crashed. A narrator gives us a behind-the-scenes look at a famous pizza shop. Are these videos part of the evening news? No, they're short documentaries! Short documentaries are non-fiction videos about real people, events and places. They're designed to educate viewers. A documentary filmmaker talks to people and visits locations to bring these interesting stories to life.

Documentary success guide

Be patient Filmmaking is something that takes practise. You won't make a perfect film the first time, the second time or ever. As difficult as it can sound, practice makes *better*, never perfect.

Keep it interesting One of the best things about making a documentary is finding a subject that really interests you. If you are passionate about something, that feeling will shine through in your work.

Capture everything When making a documentary, there is no such thing as wasted footage. Ask lots of questions and capture everything you can. Though you might not want to use everything you shoot, it's good to have a lot of options to choose from.

What you'll need:

☆ an idea
☆ a script
☆ a storyboard
☆ a subject
☆ a video camera, tablet or phone camera
☆ a microphone
☆ a location
☆ lights
☆ editing software

Filming a short documentary video doesn't need to be expensive. You can find everything you need around the house. Use what you have and capture your vision without breaking the bank.

It's all about the camera

Digital cameras

One of your most important filmmaking tools will be your camera. Find a digital camera that is simple to use and able to record long shots of video. Make sure there is plenty of room on the camera's memory card.

Smartphones & tablets

If you can use a smartphone or a tablet as your camera, you're in luck. Not only are they small and easy to use, many of them have apps for video-editing built in. If not, you can always add one. Make sure you ask an adult to help you download the app you need. And don't forget to check that there's enough memory available for all of your video footage.

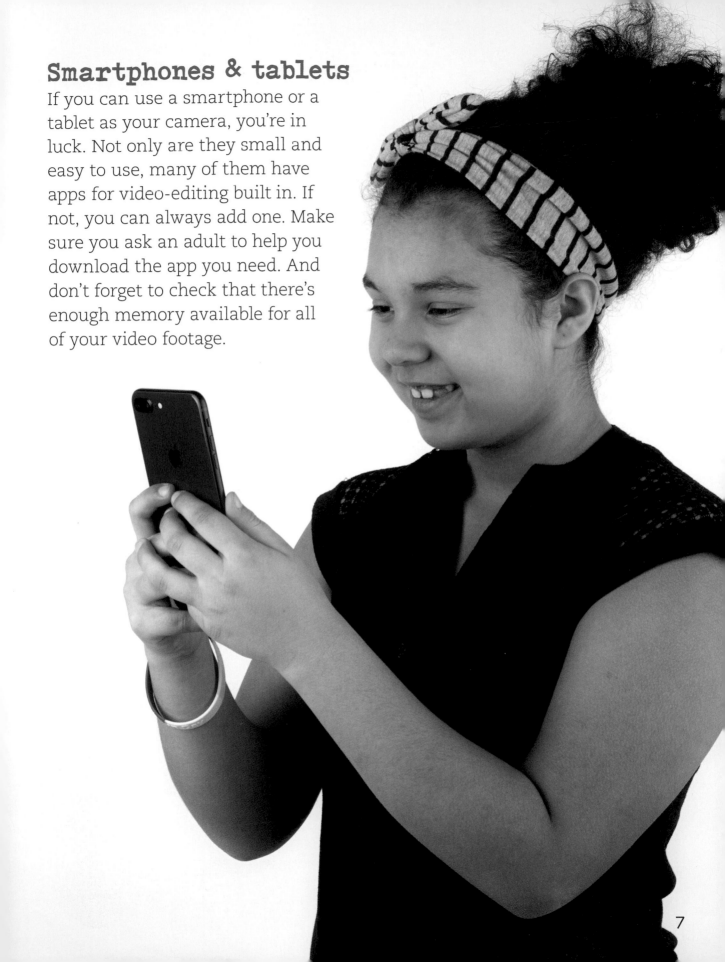

Ideas

A great documentary starts with a good idea. Pick a topic that you and others are interested in. Your community is filled with interesting people and places.

Shoot a video about the local fire station and interview the firefighters. Visit a pet shelter and learn about how they help animals find new homes. There are stories everywhere! They are just waiting to be told and shared with the world.

PRO TIP

One of the best ways to drum up inspiration is to watch some of the other (child-friendly) documentaries out there. Ask an adult to help you find some good examples.

Treatment and research

Treatment

One of the first things to do when starting a documentary is to create a treatment. A treatment is a game plan for your video. In a treatment, you write down what you want to capture during filming.

Let's say you want to film a documentary about your local ice-cream parlour. Plans can change, but having a treatment is a way to get your good idea on paper. It's a great starting point. Ask yourself a few simple questions to help guide your treatment:

TREATMENT

What is the goal of the documentary?

— The goal is to learn about how a small ice-cream parlour operates, what makes it special and how someone can open his/her own ice-cream parlour.

How will you accomplish this?

— I'll achieve my goal by interviewing the ice-cream parlour's owners/workers and doing research on the company.

Where will this be filmed?

— I'll shoot video in the ice-cream parlour (with permission).

Research

A documentary should be as factually accurate as possible. It's best to research your topic. Find as much information as you can in books, on the internet or even by talking to subject matter experts. Don't be afraid to ask a librarian for help.

Write down any information that might be useful or interesting for your audience. Giving your viewers a lot of background facts will make your film stronger. Not sure which ones to include? Think about the facts that made you say, "Wow! I never knew that!" Chances are, if YOU found it interesting, your viewers will, too.

PRO TIP

It's important to use good sources. Make sure the "experts" you interview know what they're talking about. Use facts only from reliable internet sites. News organizations and museums are good sites to use as sources. A librarian can help you determine if a site is reliable or not.

Write a script

Now that you've got a plan in place and have done some research, it's time to write a script. Using your treatment as a guide, build an outline. Somewhere in the beginning of the script, you should explain the goal of your documentary. Then plan where you'll put your facts and interviews.

Example:

Since 2001, Scoop O' Fun has been operating from my local shopping centre. Now, 18 years later, people are still in love with the ice cream they sell. In this film, we'll find out how the company started and why people are still so excited about their ice cream.

When writing a script, don't worry about making it look like a REAL Hollywood script. Describe the scene you want to shoot, who or what is there, and what's happening. Most of all, the script serves as a plan for what you hope to capture in the scene. It also helps you stay organized. There's nothing worse than finishing up and realizing you have forgotten to film an important shot.

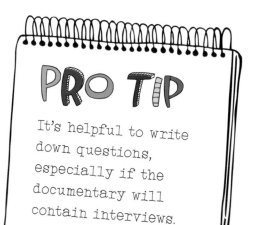

PRO TIP

It's helpful to write down questions, especially if the documentary will contain interviews.

SCRIPT

	Video	Audio
Shot 1	Full shot of the parlour's shop front. People enter the building.	Local ice-cream parlours have been around for many years. They're a popular place for summer treats. But how do they operate? What makes this ice-cream parlour special?
Shot 2	Close-up of different ice-creams on display. An assistant scoops some ice cream and places it on a cone.	We hear background noise – people chatting, the till ringing, etc.
Shot 3	Customer grabs the cone – a big smile on her face. The assistant and customer exchange dialogue.	Worker: "Enjoy your cone." Customer: "Thanks."

Draw a storyboard

Just as a script helps you organize what's going to happen and what might be said, a storyboard helps you decide how your video will look. The storyboard helps you plan where to put the camera for each shot. In a storyboard, each scene is one panel, similar to the panels in a comic strip.

scene #1

Full shot of the front of the parlour. People enter the building.

Intro narration: " ... "

scene #2

Close-up of the different ice cream in the display. A worker scoops some ice cream and places the scoop on a cone.

scene #3

Customer grabs the cone — a big smile on her face.

The assistant and customer exchange dialogue.

scene #4

Cut to wide-angle shot of the store; happy customers.

scene #5

scene #6

Don't worry about making your storyboard a work of art. If you're filming the outside of a building, sketch it! You can draw each and every shot, or you can roughly sketch what the scene might look like. The storyboard will be a checklist of the shots you'll need to finish your documentary.

PRO TIP

To make life easier, you can write notes about your audio for each shot, too. If you're going to say something before the scene begins, write a line or two at the bottom of that scene's panel.

scene #7

Close-up of owner meeting interviewer.

scene #8

Cut to owner and interviewer eating ice cream at a table.

scene #9

Interview begins.

Use prepared interview questions here.

scene #10

Cut to close-up of the vanilla ice-cream recipe.

scene #11

scene #12

Seeking subjects

Casting ☆ Subjects ☆ Actors

Now it's time to find people to be in your documentary. Make a list of the people you'd like to interview. Understand that some of them may not be available, or they may live too far away.

Can you interview someone from the ice-cream parlour? Are frequent customers available to be in your film? Finding a good variety of people to interview will make your documentary stronger.

happy customers ☺

ice-cream
parlour owner

19

Set up interviews

Using your list of potential subjects/interviewees, try to contact them to see if they would be willing to participate. Explain what your documentary is about and when you'd like to talk with them. With an adult's help, schedule a good time and place to meet for an interview.

INTERVIEW QUESTIONS

1. How long has your ice-cream parlour been in business?

2. Why do you think customers keep coming back?

3. What makes this particular ice-cream parlour special?

4. What advice would you have for someone who wants to open an ice-cream parlour?

PRO TIP

If possible, send your interviewees a list of questions ahead of time. They'll be happy to have more time to think of thoughtful answers. Plus, happy interviewees will be more likely to help you out when needed.

In some cases, you might want to meet interviewees at their homes or places of business. Again, it's best to have an adult with you to make sure you and your equipment are safe.

Pick a location

Try to find a place that's visually interesting. A blank, empty room isn't exciting to look at.

Are you interviewing an author? Film her in front of a large shelf of books or in a library. Meeting a teacher from school? Shoot the video in the classroom. Anything you can do to connect your subject to your audience will be helpful and engaging. If you can film inside the ice-cream parlour, do it. But make sure you get permission to do so, and ask an adult to go with you.

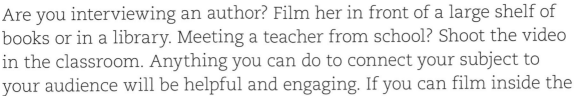

PRO TIP

Avoid white, bland backgrounds and spaces for your interviews. While the conversation should be interesting enough, it's best to have fun settings for your viewers to look at.

Light up the set

Your viewers should be able to see what you're filming. Do your best to get plenty of light on your subjects and backgrounds without making it TOO bright. Overhead light fixtures and lamps work well, but be careful with fluorescent lights. They can make people look washed out and sometimes green.

poor lighting ☹

Natural light can be a nice touch in documentaries, but the light quality will change throughout the day. That can be problematic for longer shoots. If you're doing a quick one- or two-hour scene, go for it!

PRO TIP

Take some test footage to see if you like how the light looks. If it seems too dim or too bright, make adjustments.

better lighting

25

Unless you're planning to film while walking, it's best to put your camera on a tripod. A tripod will keep the camera in place so the video isn't shaky. You can find inexpensive tripods for both cameras and phones/tablets. If you don't have a tripod, make a stack of books and set the camera on top.

← phone tripod

Decide on a good place to set up. You should be able to see the subject and background.
If you do need to go "handheld" (without a tripod), make sure your fingers don't get in the way of the lens.

PRO TIP

Don't feel that you have to keep the camera in the same spot for a whole scene. Move the camera to the side or get some close-ups. Be creative! Getting a few different angles will help keep things interesting for the viewer.

Shoot the video!

Ready to finally start filming? Perfect! With the lights, camera and talent in position, you can begin recording. If you're interviewing people for your documentary, introduce them or ask them to introduce themselves. Then you can begin asking questions that support the goal of your documentary.

Follow your script and storyboard. They'll help you stay on track and reach your goals for the documentary.

PRO TIP

Friends can help! Ask a friend to conduct the interview. Another friend can run the camera while you act as the director. The director decides on camera angles and where to position subjects.

Documentary filmmaking is different from making other types of films. Don't feel as if you need to stop recording after each question. Let the shot continue so you're not stopping and starting over and over.

PRO TIP

If you have two cameras, you can keep one on the subject and another on the interviewer. Doubling the footage will give you LOADS of options when it's time to edit.

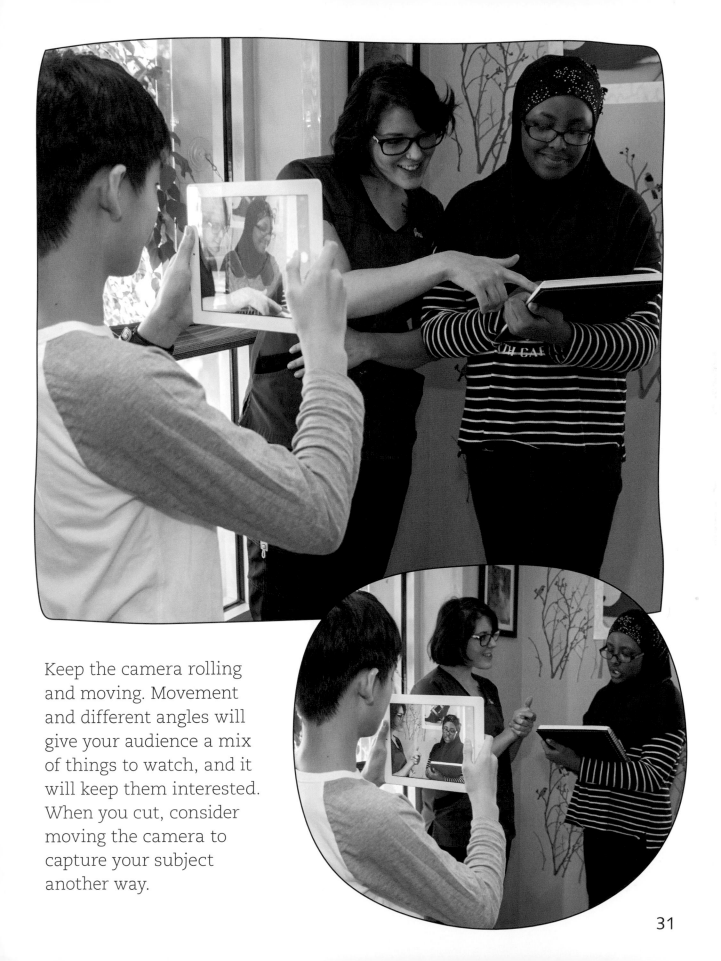

Keep the camera rolling and moving. Movement and different angles will give your audience a mix of things to watch, and it will keep them interested. When you cut, consider moving the camera to capture your subject another way.

Cutaways

Giving the audience a break from seeing a lot of talking heads is important. People tend to have short attention spans. Between interviews or topics, it's sometimes good to cut away to a shot of something else. Consider cutting away to a scenic location, an interesting object in the room, or even something you can see out of the window.

Cutaways are also great places to add narration between scenes. If you've got an interesting fact to share with your audience, an image of something different might be the best place for it.

Shot 12   Cutaway: Close-up of
          kittens in a holding
          space for cats.

Audio: Interview is taking
       place.

Miaow!

Shot options

To keep your video interesting, you need some variety! Adjust the camera, film different things in the room or film from different angles. Try these:

Pan and tilt shots – moving the camera from left to right (pan) or moving the camera up or down (tilt)

pan shot
(left to right)

tilt shot
(up or down)

PRO TIP

Capture as much as possible when shooting. Don't worry about having too much footage. You can decide what to keep and what to cut later. Having more than you need is better than needing more than you have!

34

Exterior shot – showing the location where the interview or filming is taking place; if you're filming inside a pet shelter, for example, film a bit of the outside of the building; exterior shots help your audience get a clear sense of the location

Close-up – getting up close and personal to the person, object or place you're filming

Zoom – using the built-in zoom feature to move closer to (zoom in) or further away from (zoom out) the object you're filming; this is sometimes a sliding bar or a button on a digital camera

wide-angle
(pull camera back)

Wide-angle – pulling the camera back so more of the scene can be seen

Cut it up

Rough cut

Once you've shot everything in your script and storyboard, it's time to edit your masterpiece. Editing is like putting together a puzzle with many pieces. You take the video clips you've shot and put them together in a way that makes sense.

First, pull all of your video clips into the editing app/software. (Check page 48 for suggested editing apps.) Using your script as your guide, put the clips in the correct order. Once all the clips you want to use have been "roughed" in, click play to watch your rough cut.

PRO TIP

When watching the rough cut of your video, be on the lookout for parts that do and don't work. Take notes, so it will be easier to work out where to make edits.

Cutting

Now comes the hard bit. It's time to get rid of the things that don't work well. You don't want your documentary to be too long. The key is to keep people interested. Don't bore your viewers!

Is there a long pause between questions? Cut out the extra space. Is there a clip that just doesn't seem very interesting? Say goodbye! If you don't like something in your documentary, don't be afraid to get rid of it.

☒ Cut the time
between questions in this clip.

Oops! Delete this clip. 🐱

Cute! Use this clip for a cutaway. 🐾

PRO TIP

Add cutaway shots or extra footage between interview questions or scenes. They will help break things up a bit and will give your viewers a variety of things to look at.

39

Narration ☆ Music

Watch your freshly edited documentary. Does it seem like something is missing? It might need a couple of things. Adding some narration to the documentary will give it a personal touch. Talk about your film's topic and what you hope to accomplish with the video. Explain why you're interviewing the people in the documentary. It's YOUR documentary, put your voice on it!

Have you ever watched a film without music? It can feel flat and lifeless. Documentaries can benefit from music, too. Adding even a little bit of music to your video will add interest and make it seem more professional.

PRO TIP

Make sure that you only add music that you have permission to use. You could get into trouble for using "popular" music and may be asked to remove it!

Almost there!

When your film is edited, it's time for some finishing touches. During the course of filming, did you think of a title? Add the title to your documentary so people know what to call it. While most editing apps have built-in title generators, you could design one on your own and film it.

It's likely that you didn't work on the documentary all by yourself. Make sure you add the names of your crew to the credits. Thank anyone you interviewed or who helped you find information. As with the title, you can be creative with how your credits display.

PRO TIP

Sometimes you can add unused footage as a background for your credits. If there was a scene you wished you could've used, maybe it will work while the credits roll.

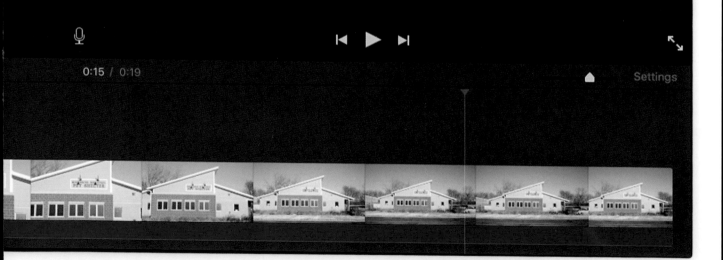

Documentary debut

Sharing your video

Now that your video is complete, you can share it with your soon-to-be fans. Make a big deal about it. You have put a lot of hard work into this! Have a premiere night at your house, and invite your family to watch it. If your friends have made videos too, turn it into a film festival. Want to see whether people around the world will watch it? Ask your parents/guardians to help you upload it to the internet (YouTube, Vimeo).

That's a wrap!

Now that you've created your first short documentary, go and make another one. Become an expert and explore a new topic. Using what you've learned, you can make something even better and more informative. With lots of practice, great things will happen. Your next short documentary will be nothing "short" of amazing!

PRO TIP

If you don't want to use your real name (or other identifying information), remove it from the video before posting it online.

JOIN US FOR A

MOVIE PARTY

World premiere
of our new
documentary!

This
Saturday
at 2 p.m.
—
Harry's
house

POP CORN

Meet your film instructor

Thomas Kingsley Troupe is an amateur filmmaker who has been making films and videos since he was at secondary school. Thomas has worked in the visual effects department for a handful of Hollywood films and shows. He has also written and directed a number of short films for the 48 Hour Film Fest & Z Fest contests and loves creating funny videos with his own sons at home. Thomas says, "Making films is the BEST. It can be a lot of work, but finishing a film to show to your friends and family is WORTH IT!"

Find out more

Books

Create Your Own Film or TV Show (Media Genius), Matthew Anniss (Raintree, 2016)

Understanding Computer Search and Research (Understanding Computing), Paul Mason (Raintree, 2017)

Website

https://learnaboutfilm.com/iphoneipadfilm/filmmaking/
Discover more good filmmaking tips and techniques.

Glossary

app computer application

documentary film about real events and people

edit cut and rearrange pieces of film to make a film or TV programme

narration speech delivered to accompany a film, broadcast, etc., to help tell the story of what is happening

rough cut first version of a film after early editing

scene part of a story, play or film that shows what is happening in one place and time

scenic creating a beautiful view

script story for a play, film or TV programme

storyboard series of drawings that shows the plot of a TV programme or film

treatment detailed summary of a film

Apps and software

Imagemaker, by the Tiffen Company – changes a smartphone experience into a more traditional camera experience

iMovie, by Apple – an app to create your own films

Movie Maker 10, by Microsoft – a full filmmaking software app for all budding artists

Index